3 STARS OF THE SAHEL AND THE AWARD FOR EXCELLENCE

3 stars of the Sahel and the award for excellence-Nẽer-songo

N° editor: 069

Legal deposit: 25-450 (June 13, 2025)

Burkina Faso National Library
Design and layout: Edition Plumes du Faso

ISBN : 978-2-38086-108-2
EAN : 9 782 380 861 082

Author's contact:
E-mail: neersongo@gmail.com

PLUMES DU FASO
Tel. (+226) 71.11.60.46/74.52.07.07
Courriel : plumesdufaso@gmail.com

Dedication

To Africa,
to the family,
to the homeland,
to the spirit of belief.

Contents

Chapter I: Three friends, one project

Chapter II: Cotton, fire, and clay

Chapter III: At Koulouba's Palace

Chapter IV: *Jènùgô*, the balafon's song

Chapter V: At the Traditional Wrestling Arena

Chapter VI: On the road to Baani

Chapter VII: *Wondudo*, the happiness of the orphan girl

Chapter VIII: Poko's speechless

Chapter IX: *Mami Wata*, the excisor of Lake Debho

Chapter X: Fighting against *Vāamba*

Chapter XI: Tassman, the little drug-addicted boy

Chapter XII: *Bishara*, the incredible news

Chapter XIII: The award for excellence

Chapter I

Three friends, one project

Ba-yiri, October 1st...

To His Excellency,
The President of the Confederation of the Great
Sahel

Dear Mr. President,

My friends Salam, Lafia, and I, Pax, are writing to you with great hope as we begin our very first step in secondary school.

We would be honored to meet you to share an idea that is very dear to us. In our town of Ba-yiri, we see far too many children living without support, scattered across the streets with no one to care for them. This has moved us deeply.

We dream of building a home for these underprivileged children. We have already decided to contribute a portion of our modest savings.

We are reaching out in the belief that you, as a leader devoted to the youth of the Great Sahel, will share our concern and support our initiative in any way possible.

Please accept, Mr. President, the expression of our deepest respect and highest regard.

Sincerely,

Pax, Salam, and Lafia

Pax, Salam, and Lafia had just stepped into the bustling world of sixth grade at the Secondary School for Excellence in Ba-yiri, the proud capital of the newly formed Confederation. They were no afraid of challenges. Ever since primary school, they had poured their energy into group projects and shared dreams. But this time, they had set their sights even higher.

One sunny afternoon, the three friends huddled under the wide canopy of a tree in Ba-yiri's beloved public space, the Mayor's Garden. The heat of the day softened beneath the branches, and they took turns reading a letter, one they had written with care and hope.

Pax's face lit up with a triumphant grin as he held up a small camera.

— At last, he declared, we can make our wish come true! We're going to shake hands with the President and take a photo with him! Are you still in?

His friends nodded without hesitation.

— Yeah, sure! We're still Ubuntu!

That word, Ubuntu, carried weight for them, a principle of unity and shared humanity, deeply woven into their upbringing.

— But how's our letter going to reach the President's desk? Salam asked, frowning slightly.

Lafia laughed.

— Good question! It's not like we're just strolling into Katreyaar market!

Katreyaar was Ba-yiri's sprawling, chaotic market, the kind of place where you could find everything and everyone.

Pax shook his head and clicked his tongue.

— Waï! The President does step out sometimes. We'll catch him one day!

Salam sighed, staring down at the letter.

— If our parents were white-collar workers, they'd just put this on his desk right now.

Lafia scoffed.

— You're dreaming! Three school kids from Ba-yiri don't just walk into Koulouba's Palace! Just being in the Mayor's Garden is already something special.

Pax stood a little taller.

— Don't forget, we're Ubuntu.

Salam tilted his head.

— Yeah, sure. One big family. But what does that even mean right now?

Pax grinned mischievously.

— It means we put our hands together bravely, because wizards are lurking!

With playful seriousness, they formed a small circle and began their ritual chant, a kind of secret oath only they understood.

Pax began, voice low and solemn:

— I am because you are!

The others followed, strong and proud.

— We are because you are!

A quiet fell over them, a stillness like the wide-open savannah, settling in their young eyes.

Then Pax, full of joy, burst out.

— Well! That's our motto for life!

His friends looked at him, puzzled but intrigued.

— Tomorrow, Pax announced, holding the letter like a treasured relic. We're going to the Palace.

Lafia gave a half-laugh, half-groan.

— Eh! I hope our pestle will match the mortar of Koulouba's Palace.

Salam stretched his arms and added.

— You know the saying. He who swallows a pestle stays up all night!

Chapter II

Cotton, fire and clay

A few days later, on the Avenue of the Cross of Zinder, Pax stepped into his father's workshop. The familiar scent of fabric and steam filled the air. He often came here to watch his father work, sewing, threading needles, and pressing garments with precision from dawn till dusk. His mother was there too, lending a hand whenever she had time. She turned to her son, who usually helped her on weekends.

— Have you done your homework? she asked, eyeing him knowingly.

— Of course, *M'mâ*! he replied.

— You're here earlier than usual...

Pax pulled a face and said, "An old man sitting down sees farther than a child standing up."

His mother exchanged a glance with her husband, just a subtle gesture, but Pax caught it and knew exactly what it meant.

— Looking for this? she asked, pulling a suit from a trunk.

He winced. He'd been found out.

— What a fine dashiki! his father said with a grin.

— You made this all by yourself?

— Yes, *Baba*! Pax replied proudly.

— For once, you haven't wasted my cotton.

Pax gave a sly smile.

— The child who listens today will be the old man

who speaks tomorrow.

He clutched his precious outfit and walked out of the workshop, his bundle held tightly to his chest.

* *

*

Across town, near the Place of the Battle of the Rail, Salam was in his father's forge. The air pulsed with heat as embers crackled in the glowing hearth. The bronze was ready. With practiced hands, he pulled it from the fire, shaping it into a bracelet. The metal hissed and cooled as Salam polished it with care.

His father watched with quiet pride.

— You're gifted, *bi-songo*, he said. Very skilled.

— I can't wait to show my friends this *zûuri*, Salam replied. They said I couldn't make anything with fire.

— If you can stand the flames, his father said, you'll warm yourself with the embers. You'll do great things, little blacksmith.

Salam wrapped the bracelet in cloth, his eyes shining, and stepped out of the forge.

* *

*

Near the Independence Monument, Lafia's
mother ran a small pottery studio where she shaped
and displayed clay pots. That evening, Lafia emerged
from the workshop, hands and arms smeared with
clay.

— There you are at last! her mother called, mid-
conversation with a customer. What are you
hiding behind your back?

Lafia stepped forward, beaming. *M'bamousso*, here
it is, she said, revealing a small clay pot.

The customer's eyes lit up. What a marvel! Such a
lovely *bogodaga!*

She admired it with wonder.

— I'll take it right now!

— Sorry, Madam... this one's already spoken for,
Lafia replied.

Her mother chuckled.

— Lafia, you're a fine *dagadala!* But you used a bit
too much clay. You'll be making the next
batch yourself.

— I'd love to! Lafia said, gently cradling the pot.
A girl is like pottery. You shape her while she's
still soft.

At Koulouba's Palace

That morning, the trio met at the United Nations roundabout. They paused for a moment to admire the giant globe, a vivid reminder of their last geography lesson. Pax and Salam wore carefully chosen, elegant outfits, while Lafia radiated confidence in a colorful dress that matched the precious parcel they carried with them.

They hopped into a taxi that cruised past the famous Filmmakers' Square.

— Where to? asked the driver.

— To Koulouba's Palace, please! Pax announced grandly.

— The Palace? Koulouba's? the driver repeated, raising an eyebrow.

— Yes! they answered in unison.

The driver chuckled. Allright then! Ever been up that high before? Hope you don't get dizzy. That'll be 100 cowries each.

— That's all our savings! they groaned, digging into their pockets reluctantly.

When they finally arrived at the grand gates of the presidential estate, they approached the guards standing in formation.

— Good morning, soldiers! Pax greeted cheerfully.

— We're not soldiers, we are *Tapsobendâmba*, one corrected sternly. Palace archers.

— *Tapso…* what? Lafia asked. Do you shoot
   arrows at kids too?

— We're the official Palace Guards, the man
   replied, unamused. Now, what are you doing
   here?

— We're here to see the President! they said,
   almost in chorus.

The guards exchanged skeptical looks.

— And why would the President want to see you?

Pax stepped forward with confidence.

— *Tapso*-men, sorry… guardians of our President,
   we have very serious reasons for coming.

Salam and Lafia nodded, standing tall behind him.

— This is Salam, son of His Majesty *Naaba-
   Vineyam* of Ba-Yiri, Pax declared.

Salam offered a respectful bow.

— She's the reigning Miss Culture from the
   Secondary School for Excellence, he added.
   Lafia curtsied and proudly held up their
   carefully wrapped gift.

— And I, Pax concluded, ranked first across the
   entire Confederation in the sixth-grade
   entrance exams!

The *Tapsobendâmba* looked them over, struggling
to hide their amusement.

— Well now, quite the distinguished guests, one
   of the guards said, half-joking. So, what exactly

do you want with the President?

— We've brought an urgent letter and a *dokkal,* a
    small gift, Lafia explained.

— Is that all? We'll deliver it for you.

— What? Tapso-men! Salam protested. We'd
    rather deliver it ourselves!

Lafia stepped forward again, addressing them
directly.

— Surely the Lady of Koulouba would love to
    receive such a fine *dokkal,* wouldn't she?

The guard cracked a smile and turned to his
superior.

— The lady of Koulouba would certainly be
    pleased.

But the leader of the guards had heard enough.

— This isn't a daycare. You've wasted enough of
    our time. Move along!

* *

*

Later that day, the trio regrouped in the city
center, wandering through the narrow alleys until
they stopped in front of the Comrade Captain
Monument, a towering bronze figure known as "The
Revolutionary," a tribute to the Confederation's
national hero.

— *Waï, waï*... What now? asked Salam.

— Follow me, Pax said with a grin. The little
hippo knows where the water is!

They made their way to the Post Office, pooled
their last coins, and bought a stamp.

— The night may last long, Lafia murmured, but
the day always comes.

— Alone, we go faster, added Salam. Together, we
go further.

They slipped their letter into the mailbox.

Chapter IV

Jènùgô, the balafon's song

On that Thursday morning, during a lively lesson on the Olympic Games, the teacher made an exciting announcement: the upcoming Sahelian Alliance Games were fast approaching. These much-anticipated sporting days were beloved across the Confederation.

— This year, the teacher declared, the Games will be opened right here in the capital, by the President himself, at the Traditional Wrestling Arena.

Pax seemed lost in thought. Salam and Lafia soon joined him.

— Are you dreaming about Africa in the third millennium? Salam teased.

— No, Pax replied with a faraway look. I have another vision. I can already see the camera rolling…

— This time, we'll get the shot! said Salam, catching on, his voice brimming with hope.

* *

*

That afternoon, the pupils were back on the field, training hard under the sun. The teacher's whistle sliced through the air, injecting fresh energy into their tired limbs.

— Just a little more effort, champions! Ever heard the *moral of the well*?

— It's with the water from your body that you draw water from the well! the pupils shouted together, their voices rising in unison.

After a final lap around the football pitch, they collapsed onto the grass.

— Don't lie around like little iguanas, it's bad for your health! the teacher called out.

A hand shot up.

— Can I ask something? Is it true that some children are trained to go to war?

Another voice followed, hesitantly.

— Could you explain how that happens? How can children end up on battlefields?

— They're called child soldiers, the teacher said gravely. And yes, it's a real tragedy.

— Do they have to fight just because the adults send them? a girl asked, casting a knowing glance towards the boys.

— And what happens to the children whose mothers abandon them? a boy added quietly.

— It's not about boys or girls, another girl responded firmly.

The girls clustered to one side, and soon, a heated discussion broke out. Voices clashed, not out of anger, but from the urgency of their shared concern.

— There's no point in blaming one side or the other, the teacher said calmly. In every case, it's about harm done to human beings.

— *Wênde!* sighed Lafia. That's what happened with the Senegalese riflemen…

— Exactly, said Salam. My father told me about them. Sub-Saharan soldiers, many were taken to fight in the World Wars to free Europe.

At that moment, Pax stood up before the group. All eyes turned towards him as he reached into his pocket and unfolded a small sheet of paper. He read aloud, his voice steady and full of heart:

Africa, sow your seeds, without being wretched,
Go forth, intrepid and unshackled!
Men from here, women from elsewhere,
Let all your beautiful flowers bloom anywhere!

Blessed land of the Sahel, proud and honest,
Don't give up on lean days, there is no rest!
Tomorrow your hands will be full of goods,
For which you've waited all night in the woods!

Look at the pink dunes of Koyma and their free wings,
On the shores of Lake Bam, the gardens of kings!
Your sun will shine on Mount Indukal,
In the Tenere, a forest will grow like as a miracle!

A cheer erupted from the group as Pax finished.

The teacher applauded and stepped forward, asking to see the poem.

> — That's my *Jènùgô*, Pax said with a bow. Like the balafon, it sings of hope for Africa.

> — It takes a whole village to raise a child, the teacher said warmly. We'll remember this poem. And good luck to all preparing for the Games!

Salam and Lafia leaned in close to Pax and

whispered with bright eyes.

> — We hope your *Jènùgô* will one day make us sing in front of the President…

Chapter V

At the Traditional Wrestling Arena

The Traditional Wrestling Arena was overflo-wing with energy that day. A sea of young people had taken over the field and packed the stands, their voices buzzing with anticipation.

Among them were Pax, Salam, and Lafia, each dressed in their finest athletic gear, eager to compete in the various events. But more than the races, their eyes were drawn to the officials' stand, said to be reserved for the President himself.

— How do you plan to get there? Lafia asked, as she eyed the restricted area.

— I've given the camera to a guy, Pax whispered, grinning. When the official delegation arrives, we'll slip into the guard of honour. When the President reaches our row, we'll shake his hand, and our guy does the job.

— *Na wodi!* exclaimed Salam, thrilled at the plan.

Half an hour later, a voice boomed through the megaphone, announcing the arrival, not of the President, but of the Minister for Youth and Sports.

The Minister extended his best wishes for a successful sports day and a joyful holiday season.

— May today's lucky winners be tomorrow's champions!

The trio exchanged glances, speechless.

— Total flop! Pax muttered.

— No guard of honour. No President. No photo,

Lafia sighed, ticking off each disappointment on her fingers.

— I really thought today was our moment, Pax groaned. This arena was supposed to be our stage!

Lafia raised her hands dramatically to the sky.

— Well, all we've got left to run with… are our legs!

The line caught them all off guard, and they burst into laughter. Just then, the loudspeaker sounded again: "All candidates, please proceed to your starting areas. The first trials begin in five minutes. Do Africa proud!"

— Which Africa? Pax muttered. A real African leader keeps his promises.

— Especially one who calls himself Pan-African! added Salam.

— Pan-Africanism isn't just speeches, it's what happens out there, on the field, Lafia chimed in.

— And this won't be an easy match! she added.

— The slave who never stands will always eat off the floor, Pax said, echoing an old proverb.

— What we're about to do… it's a fight for freedom in its own way. But that's another matter!

— Or maybe it's *this* story, Salam said, his voice

rising with passion. After slavery, colonisation, and fake independence, we're finally talking about sovereignty!

— Rise and shine, Africa! And first things first, Confederates, on your marks… let's go!

With that, Lafia bolted towards her starting point, the others close behind.

The renovated Traditional Wrestling Arena gleamed in vibrant colours, a fitting stage for what felt like the beginning of something bigger. The youth of the Confederation had arrived, and they were hungry for high-level competition.

By the end of the day, Pax had claimed victory in the 100-metre race. Salam soared to first place in the triple jump. Lafia dazzled everyone with her winning floor gymnastics routine.

Yet, during the trophy ceremony, their smiles seemed curiously subdued. When asked why they looked so serious, they answered honestly.

— We were expecting a great cup… from a great man!

To which someone replied with a puzzled look.

— Elephants can't run and scratch their bums at the same time.

Chapter VI

On the road to Baani

The harmattan wind swept through the streets of
Ba-Yiri, cool and dry, tugging at clothes and stirring
up dust. Young people wrapped in colorful *Faso Dan
Fani* darted through alleyways, laughing and chasing
one another to keep warm as the cold stiffened their
limbs. But beneath the games and gusts of wind,
everyone had one thing on their mind: the fast-
approaching Christmas and New Year festivities.
Pax, Salam, and Lafia huddled together over a
newspaper, their eyes lighting up as they read the
latest headline.

  — Have a look! Pax exclaimed. She's going to
   Baani! The Lady of Koulouba herself… but
   without the President.
  — When you don't have a belt, you tie a rope,
   Lafia replied, smirking.
Salam snapped his fingers, inspiration striking.
  — Lafia, you'll be our centrepiece!
She gasped, placing a hand over her heart.
  — Wait… what are you up to now?
  — We all need to be ready for the inauguration of
   the new children's nursery, Pax said, grinning.

* *
*

The next morning, Salam and Pax headed straight to the school's administrative office. They went to see the secretary they liked best, one who usually greeted them with a kind smile.

— Hello, young men! she said as they stepped in.

— Good morning, Madam, Salam began. We'd like to see the headmaster.

— He's at the teachers' council. No visits today.

— But we really need to talk to him!

— Enjoy your free period. He'll be available tomorrow.

— It's about the Baani nursery opening! Pax insisted.

The secretary paused, intrigued.

— Everyone wants to be part of that! The school needs to select a girl to present the bouquet to the Lady of Koulouba.

— Exactly! And we know just the right person, said Salam eagerly.

— I'm finalising the list of candidates now. Time is tight.

— Do you know Lafia from 6th grade? Pax asked. She'd be perfect.

— I'll note her name, but the decision isn't mine to make.

— You're close to the headmaster, though…

Aren't you friends? Salam asked, tilting his head.

— I think it's time for recess, she said with a knowing smile, gently ushering them out of the office.

* *

*

On the eve of the inauguration, Salam and Pax found Lafia and brought her up to speed.

— So now you know everything," Salam said.

Lafia crossed her arms, raising an eyebrow.

— If I've got this right, thanks to you two, I'm now one of the three daughters of honour. But honestly, wasn't that bound to happen?

Pax chuckled.

— Lafia, don't get ahead of yourself. Remember, the chameleon that tries to grow as big as the buffalo bursts.

— You're going to hand the bouquet to the Lady of Koulouba herself!

Salam exclaimed.

— Do you realise what that means?

— It only happens once in a lifetime for a girl from Ba-Yiri, Lafia replied, a dreamy look on her face. I'm going to be photographed with her… But what about you two?

Salam leaned in and whispered.

— When you hand her the flowers, give her a smile she'll never forget. Then, at the end of the ceremony, you introduce us. That's our moment. We'll snap the selfie of the century!

They burst into laughter, shoulders touching.

— You know, Salam said, putting his arms around them, laughter is the shortest distance between two people.

Pax howled with laughter at Lafia's expression.

— So far, so good, right, Lafia?

She winked.

— Don't worry, you can count on me!

Chapter VII

Wondudo, the orphan girl's happiness

In the Baani district, the streets sparkled with new life. Year-end festivities had given Ba-Yiri a cheerful glow, banners danced in the breeze, and colorful decorations lifted the spirits of the townspeople. But the true jewel of the season was the Wonɗuɗo nursery. Nestled in a freshly renovated hospital courtyard, whitewashed cobblestones lined the walkways, and neatly trimmed hedges bordered the paths, creating a peaceful, almost heavenly setting.

On the day of the inauguration, the sun cast golden rays over the new building, as if blessing it. Pride filled the air, Ba-Yiri now had a nursery of national standing, and everyone knew it.

Inside the large ceremonial hall, the official program began. From a respectful distance, Pax, Salam, and Lafia spotted the Lady of Koulouba, for the very first time. She was surrounded by elegantly dressed women in *bazin* and shimmering *luilui-peende* headwraps.

Pax nudged Salam.

— She's photogenic.

— She looks just like she does on TV, Salam whispered, and Lafia clapped quietly beside them.

The Minister of Social Action took the stage, visibly moved.

— This house is a jewel of the Sahel, she declared.

— We have named it *Wondudo*, because children
who have lost their parents must be welcomed
and protected every day.

Applause erupted, and women in the crowd
ululated with joy.

A young girl stepped forward with a bouquet of
flowers. Under a cascade of camera flashes, the Lady
of Koulouba leaned in and kissed her gently on the
forehead.

— What?! Salam gasped. That's not Lafia!

— Where is she? Pax shot up from his seat,
scanning the room.

The First Lady now stood at the podium, speaking
with warmth and grace.

— I thank all the donors who helped make this
dream a reality. I have deep love for our
children. No one comes from the desert, every
child is born into a family.

But Salam wasn't listening. He had spotted Lafia
in a far corner, wiping tears from her face.

— They gave my place to the minister's daughter,
she said in a trembling voice.

Salam clenched his fists.

— It's not fair. The rich always win…

Just then, Pax rejoined them, his face troubled.

— I checked with the secretary, he said quietly.

Both friends looked at him expectantly.

— She's adopted. The minister's daughter is
actually an orphan. She truly deserved this
moment.

Lafia sniffled.

— But we missed the photo…

Pax knelt beside her.

— Lafia, today an orphan created a memory she'll
carry forever. That's worth celebrating.

Salam gently helped her to her feet.

— Let's not give up. Where there is love, there is
no darkness.

Pax added, grinning,

— And remember, the mouse's laugh is the
elephant's laugh.

— Because every laugh satisfies the one who
laughs, they answered in unison.

— Exactly! It's not about size or volume, it's
about the joy inside.

Lafia's lips curled into a soft smile. They clasped
hands, chanted their shared motto with pride, and
walked off together, ready to rejoin the celebration at
the House of Wondudo.

Chapter VIII

Poko's speechless

In the heart of Ba-yiri, the streets had transformed into a vibrant tapestry of colours. After the New Year celebrations, the pupils returned to their classrooms, which they had decorated with colorful garlands. One afternoon, as the sun cast its golden glow, Lafia noticed a girl sitting alone at the back of the classroom. Approaching her with a warm smile.

— Hey Poko, it's playtime! We're going to have some good mâasa. We like these millet cakes, don't we!

But Poko remained silent, her gaze fixed downward.

Lafia gently touched her forehead and cheeks.

— Are you ill? she asked softly.

— Leave me alone... Poko whispered, her voice barely audible.

— Please, Poko... We're good friends, aren't we?

Poko averted her eyes.

— Alright then! You know, a child who shares a meal never goes hungry!

Poko's voice trembled.

— Lafia... my aunt wants to excise me.

— What drama!

— I don't want to talk about it... Poko murmured, her hands trembling.

— Impossible! A woman who doesn't like flies has to stay away from dripping blood…

Poko's words were heavy with fear.

— She said that if I told anyone, they'd send me
to the village and they'd do it anyway!

Lafia's heart sank.

— It doesn't look good... what's she doing in Ba-
yiri? she inquired, her brow furrowed with
concern.

— She's a fish seller at the market on Lake Débho,
Poko replied, her voice barely above a whisper.

* *

*

Lafia sought out her friends. She found them near
the rocks surrounding the public rubbish dump,
preparing for their usual reptile hunt.

— Are you coming with us to find the little
reptiles? Pax asked, holding up his slingshot.

— No, thanks! Poor animals...

Salam added, shaking his head.

— It's been like that since the dawn of time! Boys
hunt and girls roast! Pax joked, nudging Salam.

— Don't expect me to roast your lizards! Lafia
retorted, crossing her arms.

— Have you heard from the Lady of Koulouba?
Salam asked.

— No, I've got news of another lady instead...

She's about to be excised! Lafia replied, her voice tinged with urgency.

Their playful demeanor replaced by concern. As Lafia explained the situation, their faces grew serious.

* *
*

The next day, Lafia ventured to the small market on Lake Débho. The pungent smells of fish filled the air, but she pressed on. Approaching a middle-aged woman skillfully handling fish, she greeted.

— Good morning, madam!

— Welcome, *poug-sada*! Would you like some good fish? the woman responded with a warm smile.

— Yes, I'd like a kilo of fresh catfish, please!

The woman studied her for a moment.

— I think I've seen you somewhere before... Wasn't it at the last Miss Culture election?

— Yes, Lafia confessed, a hint of pride in her voice.

— I'd like to congratulate you, especially because you refused to show up wearing a piece of underwear! That's a terrible thing to do in public!

— Are you talking about the swimming costume, madam?" Lafia asked, slightly taken aback.

— The name doesn't matter, *poug-sada*... You know a lot about African values! the woman replied, nodding appreciatively.

— I did it for personal reasons... Lafia murmured, her thoughts momentarily drifting.

— You owe it more to your parents' education! The last Na-basga celebration was great. The chief Naaba reminded us of our values and the blessings of our ancestors, the woman continued, her voice filled with reverence.

Lowering her voice, she added.

— Have you been excised?

Taken aback, Lafia met her gaze steadily.

— What do you intend to do with this information, madam?

The woman hesitated, then spoke softly.

— I think you have been… you can thank the heavens! You're a real woman now. And I have a niece who will be one soon too!

— How do you intend to do it?

— You're a bit too curious, *poug-sada*... Come back another time, as I have to sell my fish!

Lafia said goodbye to the woman and promised herself she'd come back, thinking firmly: 'One finger can't pick up flour!

Chapter IX

Mami Wata, the excisor of Lake Débho

That evening, as the sun dipped behind the rooftops of Ba-yiri and the market at Lake Débho began to quiet down, Lafia returned. Around her, vendors counted their earnings, the clinking of coins blending with the fading hum of the day.

— Did you do good business today, madam? she asked, stepping up to the familiar fish seller.

— Yes, the woman replied with a satisfied nod. The lake is teeming with fish right now. And thanks to the Sahelian National Bank, we still have access to loans...

Lafia's eyes caught something unusual.

— You have a bandage on your finger...

The woman winced and held up her hand.

— A sorcerer fish bone nicked me, nasty sting. But that's the risk of the trade! One day, you won't have to worry about things like that. You'll be a fine lady with polished nails.

Lafia smiled gently.

— For now, I don't have any nails to polish. I'm focused on school. A girl who tends her nails properly can offer clear water to strangers.

The woman paused and looked at her in wonder.

— You're full of wisdom, poug-sada, she said admiringly, then resumed packing her fish into woven baskets.

— That's why no one should stop *Mami Wata*

from working, she added suddenly.

— *Mami Wata*? Lafia asked, curious.

— She's the finest excisor around the lake! the
   woman said proudly.

She kept talking, her voice full of admiration. By
the time Lafia left, the woman had promised to
arrange a meeting between her and *Mami Wata*.

* *

*

The next day, tension hung in the air like the dust
that rose from the path leading to the fish stalls. Lafia
returned, this time with Poko and her friends, all
dressed neatly and walking with purpose.

When the fish seller spotted them, her expression
darkened.

— Poko! What are you doing here? she snapped,
   startled to see her niece standing beside Lafia.

— I brought her, Lafia said firmly.

The woman's eyes narrowed.

— What do you mean by this?

— I'm asking you to stay calm, Lafia replied, her
   voice even.

Just then, a woman stepped forward, *Mami Wata*
herself. But when she realized what was happening,
she turned to leave.

— You take one more step, and you'll be summoned to the police tomorrow morning," Pax said, stepping in her way.

— Traitor!

Mami Wata hissed.

— Poko, you dared bring them here?

The pupils moved instinctively, forming a barrier between Poko and the two women.

— *Mami Wata*, Salam asked, why are you doing this?

— I do it to survive, she said sharply. I've lived in Ba-yiri for twenty years with no help from anyone!

— At the expense of poor children? Pax countered.

— How many have died, because of what you do?

— I never killed anyone! *Mami Wata* shot back. This is tradition. The *bâongo* rite marks a girl's passage into womanhood. What do you children know of our ways?

The pupils fell quiet. The woman adjusted her headscarf, decorated with gleaming cowrie shells.

— A tree without roots is a dead tree, she declared.

— Maybe, Pax said, his tone sharp. But tradition becomes abuse when it hurts people.

— In any case, Poko will not be excised, Lafia

added defiantly. And if anything happens to her, our parents will take care of you.

— My father runs the Sahelian National Bank, Pax warned. Don't expect another loan if he hears about this.

— My mother's a surgeon, Lafia said. If she sees that finger of yours, she might just amputate it herself, mutilator of children!

— My dad is a police commissioner, added Salam. He'll make sure you're behind bars for life!"

Pax stepped forward, his voice firm and commanding.

— Mami Wata, this stops now. And from today, you'll join the local committee against excision.

The fish seller stood frozen, her face a mix of anger, shame, and sorrow. Then, as if something inside her softened, she turned to Poko.

— Come here, she whispered, opening her arms. No one will hurt you. I promise.

The friends watched, stunned. Pax mused.

— Strange, isn't it... Even fish cry in water, but you never see their tears.

As they left the market on Lake Débho, they carried with them the quiet pride of having done something right.

Chapter X

Fighting against *Vǎamba*

The rains arrived with full force as May opened its doors to the Secondary School for Excellence. After a lesson on environmental science, Pax stood in front of the class, addressing his peers.

— Dear friends, he began, his voice carrying authority. The rainy season is here, and with it, puddles and gullies that will soon be swarming with mosquitoes. These Văamba are like vampires!

A voice from the back of the room spoke up.

— There's nothing we can do about it! They've even set up headquarters at *Katreyaar* market!

— We'll do something about it, Pax replied, determination in his tone.

Another voice echoed.

— We don't even have quinine! We have to get insecticide and mosquito nets to fight back.

— Don't panic! Pax urged. We're going to tackle the root causes of the *Văamba* problem. Divide into three groups, and choose your team leaders.

— Yes, Captain! a student stood at attention, and the room buzzed with energy.

— Starting tomorrow, your mission is simple. Collect all the discarded cans, plastic bags, and empty bottles you can find. Patrol every nook and cranny! Pax instructed.

The pupils set off on their mosquito-hunting

mission with enthusiasm.

> — Girls! Lafia called out. Don't throw trash just anywhere! Make sure you dispose of leftovers in the bins and waste water in the designated spots!

> — Guys! Pax added. Before you play football, drain those stagnant water pools full of larvae. No mercy for the Vãamba!

As the days passed, the community came together. The fast approaching of *Tabaski*, the spirit of cooperation grew. For weeks, the campaign against mosquitoes gathered momentum. The school administration even increased the number of rubbish bins and the local street vendors pitched in. The effort became a communal battle.

The mayor was informed of a significant decline in malaria cases, and as a result, the town council awarded the Secondary School for Excellence a special prize for its role in the initiative.

In June, the school hosted a medical team for a special presentation on malaria and its impact on tropical countries. The doctors, clad in their white coats, spoke passionately about the disease, answering countless questions from the eager pupils.

They learned that malaria kills millions of people every year, and the room buzzed with concern.

One pupil raised a hand and asked.

— When will Africa have an African-made vaccine
  against malaria?
Another questioned.
— Why is Africa still lagging behind in terms of
  healthcare?
A third asked.
— Why is the media always filled with
  heartbreaking images of African children
  suffering?
— And why do the wealthy go abroad for
  treatment instead of supporting local healthcare
  solutions? a fourth voice chimed in.
The lecturers were taken aback by the depth of their
  questions.
— Well done, young people, the chief medical
  officer of Ba-yiri said, visibly impressed. You've
  raised important points that demand reflection.
  Above all, remember to maintain hygiene in
  your environment. It's the quiet key to good
  health, for yourselves and for everyone around
  you. With that, I wish you all a joyful and
  peaceful *Aïd el-Kébir*!
Salam and Lafia exchanged thumbs-up with
Pax.
— Your idea was fantastic, Pax! Salam said,
  grinning.

— Now, let's focus on celebrating the Targui sheep festival!

Pax gave a thoughtful sigh.

— But… the mayor could have asked the president to present the award. We could've had our 'click' moment.

Lafia rolled her eyes playfully.

— Exactly! That photo would've been priceless.

— We'll have to come up with more ideas, Salam said, concern creeping into his voice.

Suddenly, Pax grew serious.

— We need to put our project on hold… or at least delay it.

Lafia looked between Pax and Salam, letting her arms fall to her sides, her face showing concern.

Salam, fiddling with a pen, spoke softly.

— We have to focus on the exams now, right?

— And prepare for the cultural competitions, added Lafia.

Pax sighed, his shoulders slumping slightly.

— We'll have to change our habits.

Salam shot back with a grin.

— It's easier to cure a disease than to change a habit…

Lafia nodded. That's true. But let's not forget, habits can lull us into complacency.

They paused for a moment. Together, they

embraced the change, knowing it was the right call for now.

Chapter XI

Tassman, the little drug addict

That weekend, the three friends took a break
from their studies and met up in the Mayor's Garden.
The fresh air and peaceful atmosphere offered a
welcome escape. They sat cross-legged on the grass,
watching the slow rhythm of life at the nearby
refreshment bar.

— I just don't get it, Salam said, frowning. "How
can adults spend their whole day drinking and
smoking?

Lafia raised an eyebrow.

— The better question is *why* they do it. Alcohol
and cigarettes are like onions, they make
everyone cry eventually.

— They say adults drink to drown their worries,
Pax added, but some ones must know how to
swim.

Salam's voice sharpened.

— Some fathers abandon their families because of
alcohol!

— Especially when it turns into addiction, Pax
agreed.

— I swear, a few of our classmates are already
drinking, said Lafia. And believe me, they're not
exactly topping the class.

— The further we stay from alcohol and smoke, the
better off we'll be, Pax declared.

Just then, Salam's eyes darted to the side.

— Speaking of classmates doing shady stuff... look over there.

They spotted a boy from their school, Tassman, leaning against a tree. He noticed them too and quickly tried to hide a small packet in his hand. Salam didn't hesitate. He walked straight over.

— Tassman, what's that all about?

— How long's this been going on? Pax asked, his tone firm.

— A few weeks, Tassman muttered. But why do you care?

— You're already hooked, Lafia said, her voice edged with worry.

— Leave me alone, he shot back.

— Is that a cigarette, or something worse? Salam asked.

Pax stepped closer.

— If you won't talk, everyone's going to find out. And believe me, Lafia won't keep this to herself.

— I don't care, Tassman muttered, but he was starting to breathe heavily. Moments later, he lost his balance and collapsed.

They rushed to help him, guiding him to a shaded spot in the garden.

Catching his breath, Tassman finally spoke.

— One evening, I went out. I wanted to see what Ba-yiri looked like after dark... I found kids sleeping on cardboard boxes. They offered me glue to inhale. I got sick that night. But after that... I couldn't stop.

— You'll lose your mind doing that! Lafia exclaimed.

— Let's not panic, Pax said, trying to keep the group grounded.

Salam crouched beside Tassman. Look, I know someone, a nurse. He can help. Let us take you to him.

Lafia gently took his hand.

— I'm sorry. I misjudged you.

— If I'd followed school rules, I wouldn't be in this mess, would I?

— You're not beyond saving.

Tassman looked down.

— You think I can get out of this?

— Of course, Pax said with a calm smile. If someone washes your back, you just need to wash your face.

Weeks passed. And slowly, Tassman changed. His mood lifted. His schoolwork improved. The lonely boy from the Mayor's Garden had found his way back.

Chapter XII

Bishara, the incredible news

A week before the cultural competitions, the end-of-year exams took place. For three long days, the pupils toiled over their papers while the rains outside cooled the heavy air, turning the school into a quiet hive of concentration.

When it was finally over, Pax, Salam, and Lafia returned to their favorite retreat, the Garden of Sahel, tucked away on the outskirts of the city. They had named it Dugukolo, and with a little money they had saved, they had managed to reforest the small plot with care.

Wandering among the saplings, they admired the results of their efforts.

The rains have been kind to Dugukolo, said Lafia, gently brushing her fingers along a cluster of green shoots.

Soon, the whole Sahel will be covered in trees again, Salam said proudly, swinging his rake over his shoulder.

— I just hope it rains enough this year, Pax murmured, leaning on his spade. Do you think our baobab seeds will ever grow tall enough to give real shade?

As Salam trimmed a bush, he suddenly stopped.

— Look at this mess, used bags everywhere! he exclaimed.

Lafia grimaced as she took in the sight.

— The trash of globalisation. It's like the whole world's leftovers end up here.
— Next year, we should launch a cleanup campaign, Salam suggested. We'll call it The Battle Against Plastic Bags, clean up all of Bayiri!
— Good idea, said Lafia. But for now, let's start right here. Dugukolo deserves it.
— When a tree falls, it makes noise, Pax added thoughtfully, but when a forest grows, you hear

nothing. We'll need to think about fencing this place to protect it.

—Let's start next week, Salam proposed eagerly.

—Next week? Lafia raised her eyebrows. That's the final of the cultural competitions, right after the exams!

— I don't know what you two are presenting, but I've got something in mind, Pax said with a secretive smile.

— Same here, Salam chimed in.

— Me too, Lafia added.

They exchanged knowing glances, each guarding their idea like a precious gem.

A few days before the results were announced, all pupils were called to an urgent assembly. The director stepped forward, his expression unusually buoyant.

— Our school has received news that will bring you as much joy as it brings us, he said, his voice solemn with anticipation. This is our bishara!

The crowd fell silent, leaning in.

After your outstanding work this school year, we are proud to announce that the President of the Confederation, along with his wife, will visit our school.

A wave of excitement rippled through the courtyard.

The presidential couple will attend the end-of-year prize-giving ceremony!" he declared.

Cheers erupted. Salam and Lafia jumped with joy.

— Our bishara is real! Let's warm up our djembe! cried Salam.
— Not so fast! Pax said.

His friends turned on him.

— Pax, the headmaster himself said it! declare Salam.
— This isn't some April Fool's prank! added Lafia.
— I'm not rushing to find a photographer, Pax said, half-joking, half-weary. What's the point of a calabash if it's always empty?

Lafia and Salam shot back without missing a beat.

— That calabash will stand, as long as no one breaks it.
— And don't forget, hope is the poor man's closest friend.

Pax gave a reluctant smile.

— It's not about hope or poverty, he muttered.
— I get it now, Lafia said gently. It's about faith.

With quiet conviction, they placed their hands on his shoulders.

The only cure for doubt, she said with a grin, is to believe.

The award for excellence

On the first day of July, the Secondary School for Excellence in Ba-yiri opened its gates to an unprecedented crowd. Pupils, teachers, parents, and townspeople filled the courtyard, their excitement palpable.

The morning began with a procession of vehicles, the arrival of civil authorities, and the blaring of the gendarmerie siren, signaling the start of a historic day. A new vehicle, known as the 'Sahel car,' pulled up in front of a large podium that had been erected.

The assembly watched in awe as the President and his wife emerged, greeted by a standing ovation. The national anthem resonated through the air, followed by speeches from dignitaries addressing the eager crowd.

Amidst the ceremony, the school secretary approached Pax, Lafia, and Salam with urgency.

— You're needed immediately, she said. There's a message to be read and gifts for the presidential couple.

A few moment later, Pax stepped up to the microphone, adjusted to his height, and solemnly read a heartfelt welcome message on behalf of the pupils. The crowd listened intently, moved by his words.

The prize-giving ceremony commenced, continuing until it reached the 6th grade.

— And now, honored guests, we have the pleasure of presenting an unprecedented ranking since the founding of the Secondary School for Excellence. In the same class, three pupils share the same grade point average and are at the top of the list! They are Lafia, Salam, and Pax.

The assembly erupted in applause, catching the three friends by surprise.

— They had also won first prize in the cultural competition in their respective categories! the announcer continued.

The crowd's enthusiasm reached its peak.

— Pax won first prize in traditional clothing, Salam in bronze work, and Lafia in pottery!

The audience cheered wildly.

— There's more to come! These three virtuosos have decided to offer their creations to the presidential couple: a *dashiki*, a *zûuri*, and a *bogodaga djenne*.

All the pupils stood and sang a new poem: *Jènùgô*, a tribute to their unity and achievements. Salam and Lafia exchanged knowing glances with Pax.

They were then ushered to the presidential couple for a photo opportunity. Under the spotlight, they were marveled.

The President's wife addressed them warmly.

— I'm delighted that a girl is holding off two boys on the roll of honor! she said with a touch of humor. Enjoy your *baraaji*!

Later, during the banquet, the Lady of Koulouba leaned towards the trio. I have a feeling I've read your names somewhere...

Pax recalled their earlier letter.

— Madam, he said softly, we did something foolish a few months ago... we wrote to the President!

— Wasn't it about the underprivileged children? she asked.

— Yes, we apologize...

— I admire your audacity! she exclaimed. I can even assure you that, starting next year, I'll see how feasible it is.

A ray of sunshine illuminated their faces.

— But be sure to write your address before posting the letter...

Pax reflected inwardly: *Would the President have replied if we hadn't forgotten to mention our address?*

She turned to her husband and spoke discreetly. The President looked at the three winners with a broad smile and asked each of them, as if to put them to a final test.

— What does 'Pax' mean?

— Peace! Mr. President.

— And 'Salam'?

— Peace! Mr. President.

— And 'Lafia'?

— Peace! Mr. President.

— What a treasure trove of knowledge! the President exclaimed. You will be peacemakers in our Confederation! Peace is like a flower. Always remember, you don't pull a flower to make it grow. You water it...

Lafia recalled her grandfather's favorite proverb.

— We were taught that the tree of peace has bitter roots, but its fruit is sweet!

The Lady of Koulouba looked at her with admiration.

— I've just had a little idea. I'm going to set up a Foundation that will contribute to the well-being of the children of Ba-yiri. I thank God for having been inspired by three magnificent stars!

* *

*

As the day drew to a close, the pupils gathered in the schoolyard, watching proudly the prize-giving ceremony. They were happier than ever, on the eve of their holidays.

When the report concluded, Salam remained transfixed by the screen.

— Lafia, pinch me, please...

— Why? You're old enough to do it yourself!

— Just to convince me that I'm not dreaming!

Someone in the audience shouted.

— Take a look! It's the General Secretary of S.A.N.O! He'll soon be laying the foundation stone for a youth library in Ba-yiri. It's going to be the largest one in Africa!

The news sparked a flurry of conversation.

— What's S.A.N.O?

— It's the new Sovereign African Nations Organisation!

— What do you mean by sovereign nations? Are we going to rename the United Nations roundabout of Ba-yiri?

— Maybe... We're entering the sacred era of Pan-Africanism!

— What is Pan-Africanism, precisely?

— It's recognizing that Africa is the 'Cradle of Humankind!

— Is this not a commitment to a free and prosperous Africa?

The trio listened intently to these debates. They joined hands and, with candor in their eyes, said at the same time.

— How about another bet?

THE END

Afterword

With this book, the author introduces a fresh literary form that defies conventional categorization. It is neither strictly a novel nor a tale, though it retains the elements of both. Instead, it ventures into new territory, a narrative form that blends the traditional with the modern, the written with the oral, the local with the universal.

At the heart of this style lies deep inspiration drawn from African languages and storytelling traditions. It reflects the richness of a hybrid literature, one that springs from the crossroads of cultures and thrives in the confluence of diverse modes of expression.

This book is best understood as a fusion of worlds: a literary intersection where the French-language novel meets the *solemde*, an African narrative form deeply rooted in sub-Saharan oral traditions. The *solemde* is more than just a tale, it is a dynamic, multifaceted story woven from different narrative threads, enriched with proverbs, aphorisms, and the spoken wisdom of generations.

The author names this blend the *Novel-Solemde:* a genre that combines the narrative structure of the Western novel with the rhythm and depth of African oral literature. The storytelling voice in this work is anchored in this modern African literary form, which gives rise to a new style coined in the moore language: *Rù-lemde.*

Rù-lemde, composed of the words *rù* (to climb) and *lemde* (chin or beard), symbolizes a journey, an upward path towards courage, clarity, intelligence and maturity.

In the end, this narrative is more than just a story. It is an initiatory journey, a literary quest for wisdom, a passage from innocence to understanding, guided by the quiet force of tradition and the evolving voice of modern African identity. It would be interesting to have a continuation of the story of these determined pupils, still written in the same *Rù-lemde* literary style.

The publisher

www.ingramcontent.com/pod-product-compliance
Lightning Source LLC
LaVergne TN
LVHW050927200726
843508LV00011B/2282